Stay Awake, Sally

Mitra Modarressi

G. P. Putnam's Sons

G. P. PUTNAM'S SONS
A division of Penguin Young Readers Group.
Published by The Penguin Group.
Penguin Group (USA) Inc., 375 Hudson Street, New York, NY 10014, U.S.A.
Penguin Group (Canada), 90 Eglinton Avenue East, Suite 700, Toronto, Ontario, Canada M4P 2Y3
(a division of Pearson Penguin Canada Inc.).
Penguin Books Ltd, 80 Strand, London WC2R 0RL, England.
Penguin Ireland, 25 St. Stephen's Green, Dublin 2, Ireland
(a division of Penguin Books Ltd.).
Penguin Group (Australia), 250 Camberwell Road, Camberwell, Victoria 3124, Australia
(a division of Pearson Australia Group Pty Ltd).
Penguin Books India Pvt Ltd, 11 Community Centre, Panchsheel Park, New Delhi - 110 017, India.
Penguin Group (NZ), 67 Apollo Drive, Mairangi Bay, Auckland 1311, New Zealand
(a division of Pearson New Zealand Ltd.).
Penguin Books (South Africa) (Pty) Ltd, 24 Sturdee Avenue, Rosebank, Johannesburg 2196, South Africa.
Penguin Books Ltd, Registered Offices: 80 Strand, London WC2R 0RL, England.

Manufactured in China by South China Printing Co. Ltd.
Design by Marikka Tamura.
Text set in Garamouche.
Library of Congress Cataloging-in-Publication Data available upon request.
ISBN 978-0-399-24545-9
3 5 7 9 10 8 6 4 2

With thanks to Tezh and Mom

It's time for bed,
I'm ready to go.
I asked Mom and Dad,
But they said . . .

"NO!"

"The night is still young!
Come play," they both said.
"Stay awake, Sally.
Don't go to bed."

"I'm done for the day
And so are my bears.
I'm too tired to play,
I'm going upstairs.

"Tomorrow's a school day,
I must get some rest.
If I don't sleep now,
I can't do my best."

"Oh, school! Pish posh, dear.
There are cookies to bake . . .

And brownies

and muffins

. . . A six-layer cake."

"I'm brushing my teeth.
I don't care what you say!
I'm not up for baking—
I'm too tired to stay."

"Tired? That's silly!
You're being no fun.
There are toys to be played with,
There are games to be won."

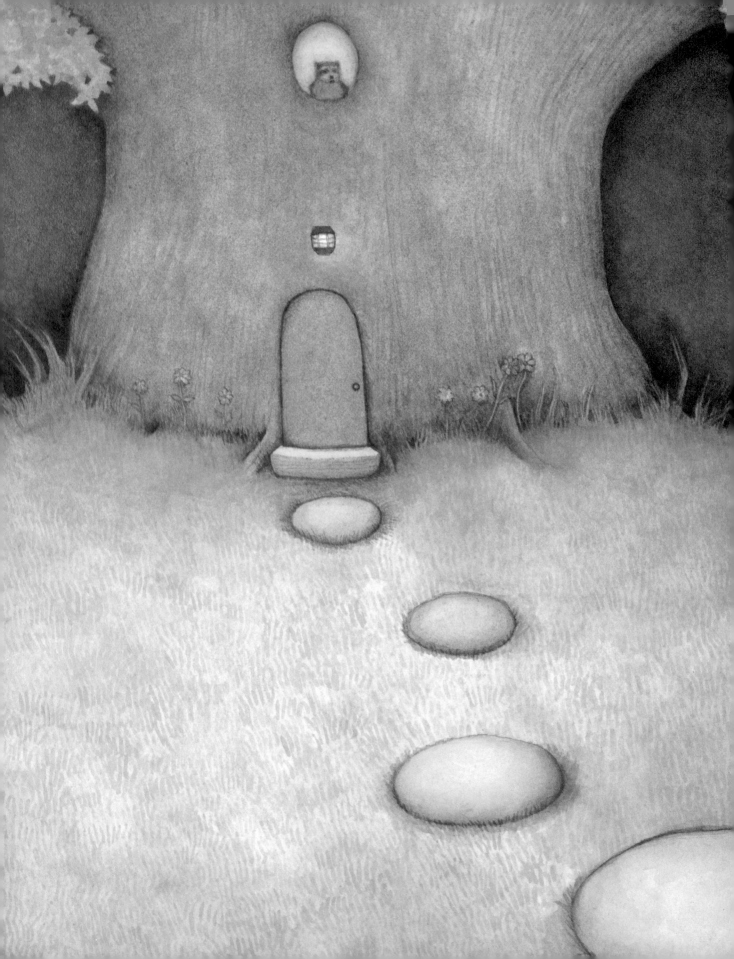

"Let's listen to music!
Let's dance in the yard!
Stay awake, Sally.
It isn't that hard."

"It's time for my bath.
I must wash my hair.
No music! No dancing!
I won't go out there.

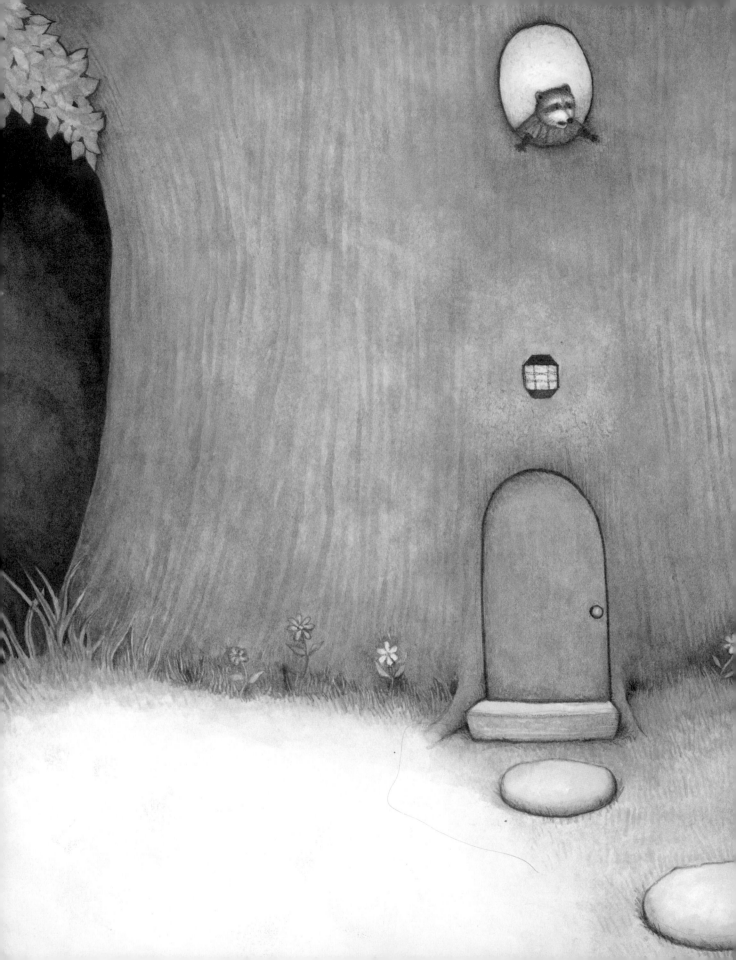

"I'm in my pajamas.
It's bedtime for me!
I'm tired and I'm sleepy,
You must let me be."

"You can read me one story."

"One story? Choose four!
Stay awake, Sally,
Just a few minutes more!

"We're having such fun,
   We can't say good night."
"But my eyes are closing!
   Please turn out the light."

"Would you care
for some water?"

"Are you sure
you're well-fed?"

"Shall we check for a monster
Under your bed?"

"ENOUGH!"

I cried out.
"You'll just have to go.
I love you a lot,
But my answer is no."

"All right, all right," Mom said
 With a sigh.
"If you really insist, we'll
 Say a good-bye.
We'll tuck you in bed,
We'll turn out the light.
You can sleep, Sally.
We love you—

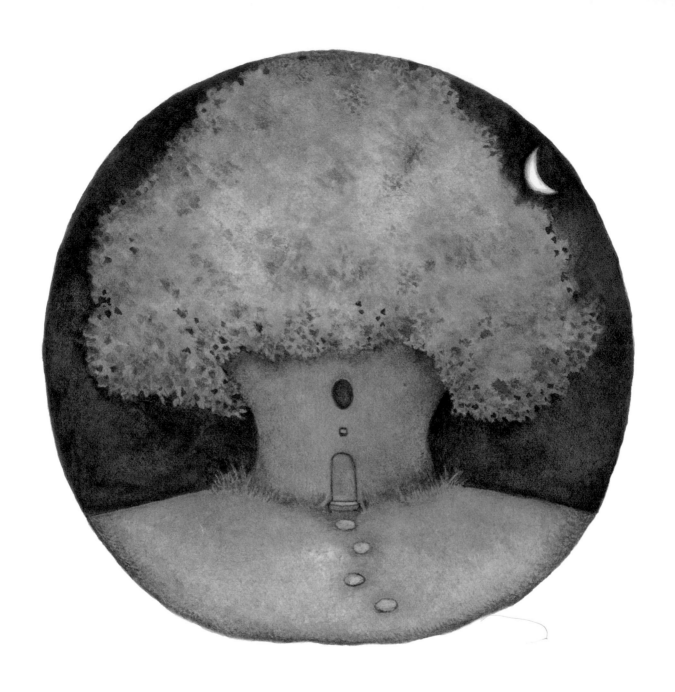

"Good night."